NO REST FOR
THE HEROES

'8-bit Jestro', 'The Book of Hiccups' and 'Tropical Troubles'
written by John Derevlany and Mark Hoffmeier

LEGO, the LEGO logo, the Brick and Knob configurations, the Minifigure
and NEXO KNIGHTS are trademarks of the LEGO Group.
©2016 The LEGO Group.

 Produced by AMEET Sp. z o.o.
under license from the LEGO Group.

AMEET Sp. z o.o.
Nowe Sady 6, 94-102 Łódź
ameet@ameet.pl
www.ameet.pl

www.LEGO.com

LADYBIRD BOOKS
UK | USA | Canada | Ireland | Australia | India | New Zealand | South Africa
Ladybird Books is part of the Penguin Random House group of companies
whose addresses can be found at global.penguinrandomhouse.com.
www.penguin.co.uk   www.puffin.co.uk   www.ladybird.co.uk
Distributed by Penguin Books Ltd, 80 Strand, London, WC2R 0RL, UK
Penguin Australia Pty Ltd: 707 Collins Street, Melbourne, VIC 3008
Penguin New Zealand Pty Ltd, 67 Apollo Drive, Rosedale, Auckland 0632
Please keep the Penguin Books Ltd address for future reference.
First published 2016
Copyright © The LEGO Group, 2016

ISBN 978-0241-27330-2
Printed in Poland – 001

Item name: LEGO® NEXO KNIGHTS™. No Rest For the Heroes
Series: LNR
Item number: LNR-801
Batch: 01/GB

NO REST FOR
THE HEROES

CONTENTS

WELCOME TO KNIGHTON . . .

... An incredible land inhabited by the brave and dashing NEXO KNIGHTS™ heroes! This merry crew protects the whole of Knighton from dark forces trying to conquer the realm. They fight with honour, valour, friendship ... and a gigantic arsenal fuelled by digital magic!

CLAY
One glance at this fellow is all you'll need to realize he's the 'knightest' of all knights!

AXL
First you'll hear smacking, then you'll see a mountain of muscles and you'll know you've just met Axl!

MACY
Instead of attending lavish parties dressed in exquisite gowns, Macy prefers clubbing ugly beasts whilst clad in a shiny suit of armour. She's a true princess, nonetheless.

LANCE
Rich, famous, charming, handsome, gallant, elegant, fashionable ... yep, that's him! If he wrote the list himself, we'd need another page. Or another book.

AARON
He can fly on his shield as if it's a skateboard with wings, and his cockiness is second only to his perfect accuracy.

MEET THE HELPERS . . .

Even the greatest of knights need a helping hand every now and then. And sometimes those hands are around for the stickiest of situations. Besides, life without sidekicks wouldn't be half so much fun!

MERLOK 2.0

He's the greatest digital magician in the whole kingdom . . . maybe because he's also the only one in the whole kingdom!

ROBIN AND AVA

The stars of the Knights' Academy, Robin and Ava are know-it-alls of constructs, megabits, terabytes, matrices, pixels, software . . . basically nerds in armour!

SQUIREBOTS

These faithful robot squires cook, train and maintain their knights' equipment. All in a day's work!

AND THE TRICKSTERS!

A word of advice: don't eat out with these guys, don't discuss the weather with them, don't even ask them what the time is – they don't wear watches. Generally speaking, only approach if you're wearing thick armour!

JESTRO

So far his career choices have been a knight and a jester. He failed miserably at both. Now he's trying to master being really, really EVIL!

THE BOOK OF MONSTERS

This gobby, magic- and monster-filled book is a true pain in the neck for the whole kingdom!

MONSTERS

Disgusting creatures imprisoned in the pages of the Book of Monsters, they do its bidding as brazenly as possible. Some of them might look funny ... but you wouldn't like their jokes.

8-BIT JESTRO

'Oh no! Not again!' Jestro cried, as the cliffs of Bonewall Canyon lit up with a dazzling display of digi-magic.

The voice of Merlok 2.0 seemed to echo everywhere. 'NEXO Power: Backlash Lightning!'

Brilliant beams of NEXO Power streamed down on to the shields of the NEXO KNIGHTS team. Suddenly their armour glowed fiercely, as their weapons obliterated any nearby monsters. Jestro saw a devastating lightning bolt bouncing among the monsters.

'Yeeeowwww!' Jestro yelled, as he fled with the Book of Monsters.

'Run awayyyyy!'

Later that night, hiding in a grove of the Deep, Dark Woods, Jestro griped about the Knights and their NEXO Powers. 'I need some magic digi-powers too!'

'Don't look at me,' the Book of Monsters grumbled, as he leaned against a fallen tree. 'I'm completely analogue.'

'I see you're on a log,' Jestro muttered. 'Tell me something I don't know.'

'No, *ANALOGUE* as in *not digital*. I'm just parchment and magic,' said the Book, flipping his pages. 'You want fancy digi-magic downloads, you'll have to become all computerized – like that insufferable Merlok 2.0.'

'That's it!' Jestro shouted excitedly. 'I'll become . . . JESTRO 2.0!'

'Tech? BLEURGH!' the Book snorted. 'Do what you want, but I'm staying here to do my scheming and plotting the old fashioned way – with pens, paper and lots of evil grinning.'

Over the next few days, Jestro made the monsters steal a variety of old computer gear left outside the Fortrex by Ava. They then proceeded to *hack* the equipment . . . literally smashing it with their clubs and swords. They're monsters after all – not computer engineers!

'Looks like it's coming along nicely!' Jestro said proudly (and cluelessly).

Later that week, the Knights found themselves by the white cliffs of Bonewall Canyon once again.

'Did Jestro REALLY send us a written invitation to re-do battle here?' Macy asked.

'Yep. That's his handwriting,' said Clay, holding up a piece of parchment covered with Jestro's child-like scrawl. 'And he even misspelled "u dum nites".'

'No, YOU'RE the dumb Knights!' Jestro corrected, as he sprung out from behind a nearby rock with his monsters. He quickly flipped a switch on the computer gear that his monster techies had been smashing with their clubs.

'Hey, isn't that the ancient junk we put outside for the garbage squirebots to pick up?' Ava asked as she peered out a window of the Fortrex.

The ancient junk projected a weird, flickering holographic image into the air. It vaguely resembled Jestro, but was all blocky and stiff-looking, and it moved with a series of primitive BLEEPS.

'Wow! That looks like of one of those old, 8-bit video games my parents had when they were kids!' Lance noted fondly. 'What fun!'

'I know! It's adorable!' Macy squealed with delight.

'Hey!' Jestro shouted angrily. 'Stop mocking my Jestro 2.0!'

The Knights stared at Jestro in disbelief for a moment. Then they all burst out laughing. 'Hahahahahaha!'

'It's not funny!' Jestro cried.

'Hahahahahahaa!'

It was very funny. So funny that Merlok 2.0, a holographic image himself, peeked out of a window of the Fortrex.

'Why, that blocky little fellow makes me look positively HI-RES!' Merlok 2.0 declared, waving his digital arms.

Jestro stomped his feet. And then he used an old-fashioned joystick to make Jestro 2.0 stomp his feet too.

'Enough!' shouted Jestro.

'BLEEP, BLOOP!' shouted Jestro 2.0.

'Monsters! Raise your shields!' Jestro commanded.

'Prepare for . . . JEXO POWER. It's like NEXO Power, but with a J!'

The monsters looked around in confusion. 'Ehhhh, we don't really have shields,' Burnzie muttered at last.

'Well, then . . . raise your weapons. Or your horns. Or whatever. Because here comes my JEXO digi-magic download: The Big Bad Blocks of Beat-You-Up!'

Jestro used his joystick to make holographic Jestro 2.0 gesture towards the sky. Suddenly, there was a magical explosion above. For a moment, it almost looked like beams of digi-powers would rain dramatically down on the monsters.

But there were no beams, just a series of small square blocks floating down.

'What's with the blocks?' Aaron asked.

'Technically, those are "bits",' Ava explained from the window. 'They're pieces of data. Looks like there are eight of them.'

The 8-bits floated down very slowly, until . . .

'Ahh! My eye!' Sparkks said, as a bit landed gently on top of his one eye.

'Ahh! That tickles!' Burnzie giggled, as another bit went down his back.

The remaining bits plinked gently on to the other monsters' heads, like blocky feathers. But it left them very confused, tickled and irritated, and they began to panic and flee wildly.

Without his army, Jestro suddenly realized that he would have to face the five powerful Knights alone. So he fled wildly as well.

Jestro dragged his computer gear behind him as he stumbled and hopped over the boulders in his path, making it look like holographic Jestro 2.0 was also running and doing old-fashioned, video-game-style leaps over objects in his path.

'Run awayyyyyyyy!' cried Jestro.

'BLEEP, BLEEP, BLOOP!' cried Jestro 2.0.

Back in the depths of the Deep, Dark Woods, Jestro 2.0 finally flickered out for the last time. Real Jestro threw away the computer gear and found the Book of Monsters waiting right where he had left him.

'Rough day?' the Book asked.

'Ughh,' Jestro groaned, collapsing onto a nearby fallen tree. 'I should've stayed on a log just like you.'

'It's ANALOGUE!' the Book
of Monsters shouted back.

But Jestro was so exhausted he had already
passed out . . . on a log.

'Oh, whatever,' the Book of Monsters grumbled,
and he went back to doing his scheming and plotting
the old-fashioned way – with pens, paper and a lot of
evil grinning.

THE BOOK
OF HICCUPS

'CRUNCH! MUNCH! GOBBLE! CHOMP . . .
BURP!' The Book of Monsters was chomping his way
through a huge stack of old Ned Knightly comic books
sitting on Jestro's rolling headquarters, Evil Mobile. He
found eating all those empty calories strangely fulfilling.
'You know, for fibre-filled fiction,' said the Book of
Monsters, licking his lips,
'this Knightly guy ain't bad.
He may be a hero, but he's
still pretty cool.'

Just then, Jestro arrived
to discover the Book of
Monsters devouring his
comic book collection.

'What are you doing?' the evil jester cried. 'Those are MY comic books. Besides, you're eating too fast! You're gonna get . . .'

The Book of Monsters stopped eating. He felt funny all of a sudden. There was a rumbling in his booky belly.

'Oh. Yeesh,' said the Book. 'I feel like I gotta . . . HICCUP!' He let out a big hiccup and – BOINK! – out popped a Globlin monster.

'The hiccups,' said Jestro, finishing his thought. 'You can't gulp your food, or in this case MY comic book collection, so fast.'

'Moan, moan, moan,' said the Book of Monsters. 'It was just a burp, not a . . . HICCUP!' The Book of Monsters hiccupped again and two more Globlins popped out of his mouth. He looked a bit worried. 'Now what?'

'Oh, I know how to get rid of these,' said Jestro, quickly clamping the Book of Monsters' mouth shut with his hands. 'You gotta hold your breath.'

The Book of Monsters struggled and squirmed, but Jestro held his mouth shut, hoping it would stop the Book's hiccups. After counting to twenty, Jestro finally let go.

'GASP! Ah, what was . . . HICCUP!'

It hadn't worked. The Book of Monsters hiccupped out a whole batch of Scurriers, who quickly scurried off towards the nearby village of Bucketon. Jestro looked worried.

'Hey, how are we gonna pillage that village if you're too busy with the . . .'

'Hiccup, hiccup, hiccup!' The Book of Monsters hiccupped out a load more Globlins and the Beast Master.

'You're askin' me?' the worried Book replied. 'I can't control my . . . HICCUP!'

Out of his mouth popped Burnzie.

'Hiccup! Hiccup! Hiccup!' In rapid succession, the Book of Monsters hiccupped out Sparkks, Lavaria and lots more Globlins, Bloblins and Scurriers.

'I . . . I can't . . . stop!' said the distraught Book of Monsters, turning around.

'BOO!' Jestro leaped out, trying to scare him.
The Book of Monsters looked frightened for an instant,
but then . . .

'Hiccup, hiccup, hiccup!' And out of his pages came
Moltor and Flama, Destruction Monsters, General
Magmar, Spider Globlins . . . and more!

'What . . . what are we gonna do?' said Jestro, unsure
how to command so many monsters.

'Well, sir,' said General Magmar with a touch of glee.
'Since we have all these monsters, we might as well . . .
ATTACK!' Magmar charged towards the nearby village
of Bucketon, and the rest of the monsters followed. This
was NOT what Jestro had had in mind.

'This is gonna be a total mess,' he worried. Thinking quickly, Jestro reached out and grabbed hold of the Book of Monsters' tongue.

'Whpt arf youb flooing?' the confused Book of Monsters tried to say.

'Holding on to your tongue is supposed to stop the hiccups,' replied Jestro, finally letting go.

'Hey, I think it worked, clown-boy,' said the Book of Monsters , but then . . . 'HICCUP, HICCUP, HICCUP!' Out of his pages came Loggerhead, one of the Forest Monsters, and Sharkerado, one of the Sea Monsters.

'Oh, boy, this is bad,' said the Book of Monsters. 'We can't be mixing Forest Monsters with Sea Monsters and Lava Monsters! They'll fight amongst themselves. Hiccup!' Out came more Globlins.

'Aaarggghhh! I may have to ask those goody-goody Knights for some help,' said Jestro. But as he looked towards his monsters attacking Bucketon, Jestro realized that the Fortrex had already arrived, bringing the NEXO KNIGHTS team with it.

In Bucketon town square, Clay led the other Knights in a tight wedge formation to battle the oncoming monster horde. It was lucky that they had detected Jestro's Evil Mobile before he attacked.

'Let's use wedge formation four-two,' ordered Clay. 'And keep it tight, folks. Looks like the Book of Monsters has belched up everything he had.'

'Whoa!' said Aaron. 'Jestro doesn't usually pull out all the stops like this.'

'Yeah,' added Macy. 'Is that a Shark Monster?!'

'There sure are a lot of 'em,' said Axl.

'Great,' said Lance, knocking away some Globlins. 'Now I'm gonna get all sweaty.'

Clay wasn't sure what was going on either, as he watched a steady stream of monsters rage into the town.

'Hey, uh, Ava?' said Clay into his radio link. 'Is it just me or are there more monsters than usual coming at us?'

Alarms blared in the Fortrex as Ava looked at the Control Centre view screen. It was filled with red radar blotches marking the monsters.

'Yeah, looks like Jestro threw the book at us,' said Ava. 'The whole book.'

'Massive masses of many monsters!' cried Merlok 2.0 looking on. 'We need some sort of special download to deal with all of these monsters!'

'Thanks for stating the obvious,' said Ava, still struggling to track all the monsters.

Meanwhile, in the centre of Bucketon, the Knights formed a defensive circle to try and fend off all the monsters. But, to make matters worse, the monsters

were fighting with each other as well! Sharkcrado and Loggerhead were tossing Burnzie and Sparkks into village buildings, and generally tearing up the place.

'The monsters are fighting each other,' said Macy, pointing to them. 'What a monster mess!'

'Clay! CLAY!' a voice shouted from somewhere behind the Knights. Clay turned around to see Jestro dragging a still-hiccupping Book of Monsters with him. 'Clay, you've got to help me! The Book of Monsters has the hiccups and he keeps spewing out monsters!'

'HICCUP! HICCUP! HICCUP!'

More monsters were burped out of the Book of Monsters. He was getting worn out!

Clay called in to Merlok 2.0 in the Fortrex.

'Merlok,' said Clay through the view screen, 'the Book of Monsters has the hiccups and he's bringing up every monster he has.'

'Now that's weird,' said Ava.

'Great gurgling gullet! That's not weird, that's serious,' Merlok 2.0 replied. He thought for a moment, before saying, 'But I think I have the perfect medicine for the mad book.' Merlok 2.0 turned to Ava. 'Prepare for NEXO Power download!'

Back in the centre of Bucketon, Clay and the rest of the team thrust their shields up into the air. 'NEXOOOOO KNIGHTS!' A Magic Download formed over their heads.

'NEXO Power: Slime Blast!' intoned Merlok 2.0. A rush of digi-magic downloaded into their shields. Their weapons now pulsed with an unusual new NEXO Power.

'Is my lance making slime?' asked Lance, genuinely surprised.

He swung his lance at a nearby monster. The weapon magically produced a glob of slime that covered the monster, trapping it.

'Ewww! How's that supposed to cure hiccups?' Lance asked disgustedly.

'Who cares? It's slime time!' yelled Aaron on his hover-shield, as he giddily blasted the nearby monsters with his bow. His digi-arrows created globs of magic slime that completely immobilized the attacking creatures.

'It's an old magician's cure for hiccups,' Merlok 2.0 told the Knights. 'Just fill the Book of Monsters' mouth with that slime and his hiccups will stop.'

The Knights sprang into action, covering the monsters in magical slime. Once trapped, the monsters would struggle and then dissolve into a colourful, slime-covered mist. This magical slime mist then sailed back into the Book of Monsters' mouth, quickly filling it up.

'Yuck!' said the Book of Monsters, struggling, as wraithlike, slime-covered monsters jammed into his mouth. 'This is the worst-tasting slime ever! It's like I've got a mouthful of lemons!'

'Yes,' Merlok agreed, 'that's exactly what this particular slime tastes like.'

'Ah, the old lemon cure for the hiccups,' said Jestro, watching the Book's mouth fill up. 'I always forget that one. You bite something sour and it totally shocks your mouth into making the hiccups stop.'

'Huh?' the Book of Monsters asked, but his mouth was too full of sour lemon slime to say anything else. Finally he gulped all the slime down, and then made the strangest face.

Jestro looked at the Book of Monsters. He looked sick. The Book shook his mouth and squirmed. Then he took a breath. 'Hey,' said the Book. 'My hiccups are gone!'

'Great,' said Jestro. 'Then let's . . . scram!' He grabbed the Book of Monsters and they ran off as the Knights prepared to capture them.

'They're getting away!' shouted Aaron.

'That's okay this time,' said Clay. 'We left the Book of Monsters with a really bad taste in his mouth.'

'Really? Did you really just use that line?' asked Lance. 'You need to fire whoever writes your material.'

'Hey,' said Aaron. 'Don't be such a sourpuss.'

Lance rolled his eyes. 'Peasants.'

Later, as the Evil Mobile slowly rolled back to the Lava Lands, the Book of Monsters kept spitting and licking his leathery lips – 'Pi-TEWY! Yuck! I can't get this vile taste out of my mouth!'

'Well it's better than having the hiccups, isn't it?' Jestro replied.

'Yeah, I guess,' said the Book of Monsters. 'Say . . . you got any more of those Ned Knightly comics?'

'NO!' said Jestro.

Then Jestro smiled. He'd just had a great idea: maybe he'd cover all his comic books with lemon juice. Then the Book of Monsters would never want to eat them.

TROPICAL TROUBLES

The exhausted NEXO KNIGHTS heroes sailed across the sea on a sleek new Hover Sloop. Their ultimate goal? A well-earned holiday. They all nearly dozed off on the deck as they hovered over the waves.

'I'm so tired from all the fighting we've done. I'm too tired to eat,' said Axl, nodding off.

'Now that's tired,' said Clay, doing some stretching. He was pretty worn out as well.

'Are we there yet?' Aaron asked sleepily.

'No, but we will be soon . . . once we crank up that Turbo-Zurbo Super Charger that Ava installed on our Hover Sloop!' Lance exclaimed, pointing to a large red button on the boat's controls. 'She said it'll make us take off like a rocket.'

'No!' Clay shouted. 'This is supposed to be a holiday for relaxing and recharging. Not racing around.'

'Awwww . . . But can we at least stop at the island over there? The surfin' looks amazing!' Aaron pointed towards a small tropical island with luscious palm trees, white sandy beaches and a mysterious little castle in the middle of it.

'Where'd that island come from?' Clay asked, unfolding his many nautical papers. 'It's not on any of our maps . . .'

'Who cares? I see sun, sand and surf!' Aaron declared, steering the Hover Sloop towards the beautiful island.

'And a stylin' holiday castle! I am soooo there!' agreed Lance.

'Are those yummy tropical fruit trees?' Axl asked hungrily.

'Commence holiday . . . NOW!' Lance declared, as the sloop cruised right up onto the white sand. Lance, Axl and Aaron jumped off the boat excitedly.

'Wait! We don't know anything about this place!' Clay warned, fussing with his papers. 'Hold on while Macy and I research it a little more. Right, Macy?'

But when he looked up, Macy had jumped off the ship too. She was already building a little sandcastle in the sand.

'C'mon, Clay, this place is AMAZING!' she yelped excitedly. 'Enough researching! This is supposed to be a holiday, remember?'

Clay sighed and nodded.
'I suppose it won't hurt to stay just a little while . . .'

Then he joined the others on the prettiest little tropical island anyone had ever seen.

A short distance away, Jestro and the Book of Monsters watched the Knights from a small inflatable raft.

'You've just helped our enemies find the prettiest little tropical island anyone's ever seen!'

Jestro said, scratching his suncream-covered nose and adjusting his life jacket. 'I expect more when you eat a magic book.'

'Hey, that was the *Book of Travel* I ate,' the Book replied with a burp, resettling his sunglasses across his cover. 'It's unpredictable. But don't worry. Things will get interesting soon . . .'

Soft sand. Warm sun. Cool water. Even Clay was beginning to relax on the island. He eyed Macy and Lance

sunbathing on beach towels a short distance away. Across the beach, Axl devoured a pile of tropical fruits he had picked, while Aaron tore up the surf on his hover shield.

Clay turned back to his light summer beach reading – well, actually it was the Knight's Code, which was the only book that Clay ever read. But it helped him relax. Until a heap of sand flew onto his pages.

'Hey! Quit kicking sand at me!' Clay shouted. But no one was anywhere near him. 'Strange . . .'

Meanwhile, Axl reached for one of his fruits, and the entire pile rolled away. 'Hmm . . . I didn't realize this island was so tilted.'

Sunbathing Macy and Lance were also sliding down the now suddenly steep beach on their towels.

In the sea, Aaron had just caught a particularly big wave. 'Sweet!' he shouted with a grin. 'I'm gonna take this right onto the sand '

CLUNK!

Aaron slammed into an enormous blue wall where the beach had been a moment ago. The beach was now several metres above his head, resting atop the wall that was continuing to grow. 'Whoaa . . . This is one CRAZY tide.'

Just then, a massive cave opened in the blue wall. Or at least Aaron thought it was a cave . . . until the cave blinked and began to look around.

'No way! This island has an eye?'

Actually, it had two eyes. And a giant face on a head that was twice as wide as the island.

Floating a short distance away in their raft, the Book of Monsters smiled proudly at his creation. 'Behold the Behemoth of Brine,' the Book said, peering over his sunglasses. 'I can pull many kinds of monsters from my pages. Lava Monsters, Magma Monsters – even Sea Monsters. The Behemoth of Brine is one of my favourites. Wouldn't you agree, Jestro?'

But Jestro was huddling and shivering in a corner of the raft. 'B-b-b-b-big monster,' was all that the terrified Jestro could say.

The Behemoth was so big, he was like an underwater mountain, rising to the surface of the sea. The 'holiday island' was actually just the hair on top of his head . . . where Clay, Axl, Macy and Lance were now trapped.

'Hey, this is no beach. It's the head of a monster!' Lance realized.

Suddenly the Behemoth's massive tentacles came whipping past them. The limbs were hundreds of metres long, and kicked up the sand with a ferocious wind. There were dozens of them. The Knights ducked just in time.

'A monster with REALLY long arms!' Macy shouted.

'We've gotta get off this island!' Clay shouted. 'To the Hover Sloop!'

But when they rushed off to find the boat, it was several hundred metres below them, at the base of the 'cliffs' that formed the monster's body.

'Too far to jump!' Macy shouted. She ducked as another massive tentacle whipped past her.

'We won't jump, we'll swing!' Clay shouted, as he grabbed on to one of the passing tentacles.

Macy, Lance and Axl each grabbed the next tentacle that whipped past them.

'Whoahahahah!' they shouted, as the tentacles twisted and wriggled.

'Ate . . . too . . . much,' Axl groaned. 'Getting seasick.'

'You mean sea-monster sick,' Lance corrected.

'Just a little more!' Clay yelled, grabbing on to one of the tentacles as it swept past.

And then . . . SPLASH! The tentacles hit the water.

The Knights suddenly found themselves beneath the surface of the sea, staring at the enormity of the Behemoth's body. It was literally the size of a mountain.

Precious air bubbles escaped from Macy's lips as she glared at the monster. How could they ever beat such a massive creature? She wanted to scream, but then . . .

'I've got you,' Clay said, as he pulled her out of the water.

The next thing Macy knew, she was back on the Hover Sloop with the rest of the Knights.

'I don't know about you, but I'm giving this holiday island a terrible review on KnightonGetaways.com,' Lance muttered.

Just then, two of the massive tentacles slammed down, nearly capsizing the Hover Sloop. The Knights grabbed on to the boat's deck, as more tentacles crashed down around them.

'Aaron! Didn't you say Ava gave this boat an upgrade?' Clay called out.

The shadow of crashing tentacles grew larger, as a massive limb hurtled towards them.

'Aye aye, Captain Clay!' Aaron shouted. 'Here goes the Turbo-Zurbo Super Charger.' And then he hit the red button on the boat's controls.

The sloop took off like a rocket – ZOOM! A split-second later, the tentacles crashed down onto the exact place where the boat had been!

The craft swooshed ahead of the creature, but the Knights were not out of danger.

The Behemoth's tentacles stretched great distances, smashing and splashing all around them.

The Knights clung to the deck as the ship zoomed along. Except for Aaron – he steered the high-speed craft with an excited, 'Wooohoooo!'

On the small life raft, Jestro clapped excitedly. 'Look at them – they're running away! *Run away! Run away!* I'm usually the one saying that, but today it's your turn.' Jestro stood up and shouted giddily, 'Run away! Run away! Run away!'

'Jestro! Sit down!' the Book of Monsters shouted. 'You're going to tip us – ohhhhh!'

Suddenly the Hover Sloop zoomed by them, causing the raft to tilt precariously. This was followed by the SMASH-SPLASH of the Behemoth's tentacles, which sent Jestro and the Book of Monsters flying out of their raft.

'Ahhhhhhhhh!'

The Knights were too distracted to see the little life raft, but Clay thought he heard Jestro's voice in the distance. 'Was that Jestro saying, "run away"?'

'I don't know. But it feels like we're the ones running away,' Macy replied.

'Yes, we're running away, but we're not retreating. We'll beat this beast,' Clay assured her. 'Aaron, take us in the fastest, widest, wildest circle you can imagine.'

'Aye aye, Captain Clay,' Aaron shouted.

Clay had learned a lesson in his near-defeat in the Valley of Argh. He realized that winning a battle wasn't always about power or strategy. It was also about endurance. The Knights had been stronger than the monsters in Argh, but the monsters had almost beaten them by wearing them down.

'We'll just tire this beast', Clay explained.

'Aye aye, Captain Clay,' Aaron said again. 'Oh, and by the way, I like saying that.'

'I noticed.'

It was not an easy strategy. At times the Behemoth's tentacles almost reached their zooming boat, or the massive limbs splashed so fiercely that the craft almost flipped over. But eventually the Behemoth seemed to be having trouble lunging at them. Its limbs grew tired. The creature seemed to lag further and further behind them.

The Turbo-Zurbo Super Charger kept them zooming along at full speed. The Behemoth, on the other hand, slowed to a floating crawl and eventually . . . it stopped chasing them completely. It sank its massive body below the surface, taking the mysterious holiday island on its head with it.

Once the Knights saw this, they all cheered.

'Nice work, Clay,' said Lance. 'Although I'll miss that stylin' holiday castle.'

'And those fruit trees,' Axl grumbled.

'I'll miss saying, "Aye aye, Captain Clay",' added Aaron.

Clay nodded. 'At least we got a little holiday time in. I actually feel a bit refreshed.'

'Yeah, me too. Which is more than I can say for that monster,' Macy added. 'It looks like our holiday island . . . needs a holiday!'

The Knights laughed as they cruised back to the shores of Knighton. No one noticed the soggy Jestro and even soggier Book of Monsters clinging to a floating buoy off the coast, grumbling to themselves as they shivered.

HOLIDAY SNAPSHOTS

Warm greetings from our mysterious island getaway.
It's nice and sunny here and we're having a blast…
but we're missing all the adventure a little!

GLOSSARY

BEAST MASTER
Coming from the *Book of Chaos*, he's definitely not the cool-as-a-cucumber type – more crazy-as-a-pickle, in fact! He's the proud owner of two dippy Globlins: Muffin and Poopsie, who he keeps on a chain ... and this is the only thing he does that vaguely resembles reasonable behaviour.

BOOKKEEPER
The Bookkeeper was taken from the pages of the Book of Monsters and, according to the Book, the only reason he exists is to serve, carry and listen to the Book's nasty remarks! The Bookkeeper appears to have a permanently dull facial expression, but what he's really thinking remains a mystery to everyone.

BURNZIE AND SPARKKS
These two dream of fighting alongside the NEXO KNIGHTS team, although it often ends badly for them. When they break something, they promise they'll be better next time ... but they never are – possibly because they're not the sharpest tools in the shed.

GENERAL MAGMAR
In need of an army general who's also a poet, philosopher, artist, tactical mastermind and gourmet

chef? Look no further – General Magmar is the guy for you! He'll always be willing to give you a motivational chat or share his lava cookies recipe with you – as long as you're willing to conquer the world with him!

KNIGHTON
A remarkable realm ruled by King Halbert, known for its lush forests, deserts and mountains. Knightonia is its largest city and the capital of the land, where the royal castle and famous Knights' Academy are located.

LAVARIA
'Don't trust anyone. Spy on everyone' could be her motto. She's the sneakiest agent of the Magma Monsters, and very hard to spot. Be careful what you say, she might be lurking nearby...

MOLTOR AND FLAMA
These twins are the pride of the Monster Academy. That's where they learned how to be tyrants, bullies and foul pranksters. Even though they're hot-tempered and combative, they have no trouble executing orders – as long as they're evil orders.

NEXO KNIGHTS HEROES
Valiant warriors who have finished their education at the Knights' Academy. They are the backbone of the Knightonian army. They might look like traditional knights: clad in armour and helmets with visors, and fight with old-fashioned weapons such as swords, lances or crossbows, but all their equipment is enhanced by cybernetic magic.

POWERS
A mixture of magic and cybernetics, created when the magician Merlok cast an immensely powerful spell to save the kingdom from Magma Monsters.

SHIELDS
The shield symbolizes knighthood and displays a warrior's coat of arms. In Knighton, shields are great weapons, strengthened by digi-magic. They also allow the Knights to absorb magical energy.

THE BOOKS OF DARK MAGIC
These books are pure evil and should be handled with the greatest of care. One might think books are for reading, but there's someone who likes nothing more than literally devouring them – the Book of Monsters. It turns out that if you eat evil books, you become stronger . . . but don't try this at home!

THE FORTREX
Headquarters for the NEXO KNIGHTS team. A heavily armed building which is both a fortified castle and a tank. It's also the residence of Merlok 2.0, who advises the Knights.